WOLF PACK

OF THE

WINISK RIVER

PAUL BROWN

Lobster Press™

Wolf Pack of the Winisk River
Text © 2009 Paul Brown

Published by Lobster Press™
1620 Sherbrooke Street West, Suites C & D
Montréal, Québec   H3H 1C9
Tel. (514) 904-1100 • Fax (514) 904-1101 • www.lobsterpress.com

Publisher: Alison Fripp
Editor: Meghan Nolan
Editorial Assistant: Susanna Rothschild
Illustrations: Robert Kakegamic
Graphic Design & Production: Tammy Desnoyers
Production Assistant: Leslie Mechanic

We acknowledge the financial support of the Government of Canada through the Book Publishing Industry Development Program (BPIDP) for our publishing activities.

We acknowledge the support of the Canada Council for the Arts for our publishing program.

The Canada Council | Le Conseil des Arts
for the Arts | du Canada

Library and Archives Canada Cataloguing in Publication

Brown, Paul, 1942-
    Wolf pack of the Winisk River / Paul Brown ; Robert Kakegamic.

ISBN 978-1-897550-10-6

    1. Wolves--Juvenile fiction. I. Kakegamic, Robert II. Title.

PS8603.R693W64 2009   jC813'.6   C2008-906266-3

Printed and bound in Canada.

Text is printed on Rolland Enviro 100 Book, 100% recycled post-consumer fibre.

for Janet, Catharine, and Julian

Phyllis, Carol, Lynn, Kristin,
and especially James for his unflagging support

with thanks to my editor, Meghan Nolan

and to Lynn Hatfield
and the students of Matahamao School in Peawanuck

– Paul Brown

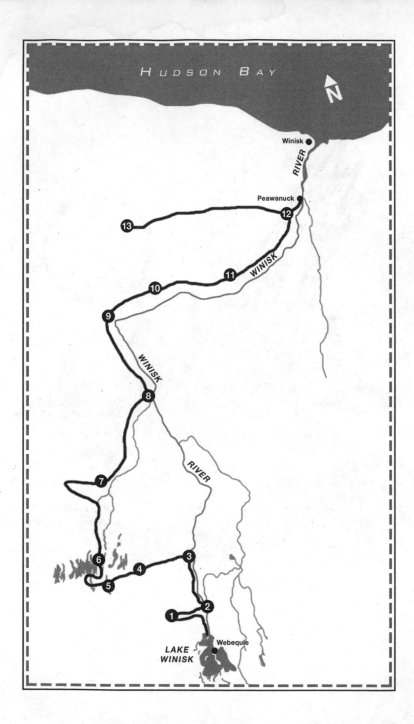

THE PACK'S JOURNEY

1 - 13: The thirteen-day journey of the pack

Day 1: A frightening kill.
Caring for White.

Day 2: A helpless moose calf.

Day 3: Raiding a campsite.

Day 4: Wolf plays a joke.

Day 5: A mysterious sound.

Day 6: Razor-sharp talons.

Day 7: Tragedy: a surprise enemy attack.

Day 8: A human pack.

Day 9: Winisk town destroyed.

Day 10: The wolves go fishing.

Day 11: Polar bear!

Day 12: Peawanuck.

Day 13: A surprise visitor.

one winter night

out of the cold dark woodlands

the wolf slips secretly into the quiet town on swift paws

beneath each streetlight
against the black sky
a white teepee
of
sparkling snowflakes softly falling

the plowed streets of the town
edged with pillow banks of sleeping snow
make easy travelling for a tough timber wolf of the North

he stops and pees over the markings of a pet poodle
and trots comfortably along the avenues

chained to a backyard doghouse
an angry German shepherd growls at him

he pays it no mind

at a corner he scans left and right

not knowing what he is looking for

but when the winter wind brings him the odour of meat

he follows the scent

at the pizza parlour on a side street downtown

all the pepperoni and bacon and sausage is out of reach

under the heavy dumpster lid

a fierce orange tomcat

sneaking away around the corner of the building

eyes him

and hisses

Wolf lunges once without real interest

and lets the tom flee

up the fire escape

he is not feeling mean

but he is not feeling happy

curious

he continues to the end of the alley

and

fearing nothing

walks slowly down the centre of the deserted main street

leaving a long single line of tracks in the snow behind him

window shopping

he finds nothing to interest a wolf

he hears

a long way off

a deep rumble

trots into the nearest alley

and waits in hiding

watching for the roaring beast

Mr. Palubiskie's red dump truck

the yellow plow on the front making sparks bouncing off the pavement

rumbles by

shaking the earth beneath Wolf's feet

a small snowstorm swirling behind the disappearing monster

Wolf has seen a moose
a deer
and even a polar bear
but nothing like this

it has no legs
yet it runs fast

after he watches it disappear in the distance
he sets off again in the opposite direction

at the south end of main street
he climbs to the top of a huge mound of snow
piled high there by a front-end loader
a good place to study this northern lumbering town

Wolf is silent standing on this white hill
no body heat getting through his woolly undercoat and thick guard fur
to melt the thickening layer of snow on his back

out of his view behind a tall white spruce across the street
a woman
restless and unable to sleep

pauses to gaze out her second-storey bathroom window

sees the beautiful wolf

and stares in fascination

he is handsome

and powerful

a huge Alpha male

one hundred and seventy-five pounds

thick salt-and-pepper fur on his back

his sides and underbelly and legs a creamy-white

his majestic bushy grey tail black-tipped

strong lean feet

the front larger than the back

compact hairy ears erect and alert to any sound

a grey mask down to his eyes

light-tan face bordered with white

an open wet black nose

some fine sense

makes the wary wolf turn and

look upward through the spruce bows

to spy the human at the frosted window

she cannot imagine

why this wild creature has entered her town

no one knows what Wolf thinks

behind the intense stare of the cold yellow eyes

centred with black round pupils

is

a

mystery

safe in her home

yet afraid

she shivers

and turns back to her warm bed and her mate

coming back from hunting one night like this two years ago

in the bloody snow Wolf saw tracks of a huge rogue black bear

and the red ripped-apart body of Wolf's mate

lying at the entrance to their den

the black bear had dug out and eaten three of Wolf's pups

but one male pup escaped

never to be seen again

because wolves usually mate for life
Wolf had not taken another female

he comes off the white hill
and continues his search
in the narrow streets on the south end of town
and smells coal smoke and wood smoke on the air
the few houses here far apart and run-down

passing a grey rusty sheet metal mailbox
he stops suddenly
catching the scent of blood
and venison

up the driveway he trots to a rough wooden garage

circling it he pees on all four corners
to warn intruders off
and finds a side door ajar

pushing the door open with his nose
he quickly locates five steaks left on top of the freezer
and devours them
butcher paper and all

in the cave-like garage
drowsy after eating
he curls up on a folded tarp in a corner
with his tail over his face
and sleeps

he is awakened in thin dawn light
by chirpy sounds
not birds
but two small pink-faced humans outside the open door
and the adult female

Wolf ranks her as the Alpha female

she makes noises he does not understand

you boys forgot to close the door
how many times do you have to be told?

she slams it shut

fiercely alert
he ranges round and round the garage
lunging at the dirty windows

no way out

he begins to gnaw at the wooden door just below the doorknob

in an hour the morning is brightening

he has a hole chewed through the door big enough to put his head through

his gums are bloody from wood splinters
his jaw muscles aching

he pokes his big head out the hole to study the situation
and hears that same rumble
the roaring beast
only not so loud this time

in a few minutes
he sees a smaller beast than the last one
following his tracks up to the garage

the roaring beast suddenly stops

bang!

Wolf pulls his head in and steps back

a human approaches

Wolf recognizes him as the Alpha male

he notices the damaged door
peers inside
and sees Wolf staring intently at him

wellwellwell

what do we have here?

how the hell did you get in there chief?

whatzamatter

hole not big enough fer yuh?

the man turns away and enters the door to the kitchen

inside
leaning his back against the countertop
drinking his third beer since getting off work at eight a.m.

he calls two buddies on his cell

bring some beers over
you'll see two fantastic things you've never seen before
and we'll have some fun

in a short time
the two in snowmobile suits
shuffle their way across the lawn from the house next door

each human
beer in hand
takes a turn peeking in at the hole

look at the size of that mother

that ain't no mother
that's a father

hahaha

out of his parka pocket
the man of the house pulls out a handgun
hands it to the bigger of his two friends

here buddy
see if yuh can get him

Jesus
where'd yuh get that?

smuggled it over the border from the States
in the wife's purse ten years ago

the big bearded man takes the Smith and Wesson
hefts it
turns the stainless steel 357 magnum over in his hand

she's a heavy brute
nice fake wood-grained grip
comfortable finger grooves

the smaller man in the green snowmobile suit
takes the brutal shining silver gun

it's a work of art man

he puts his arm through the hole and pokes his head through after

Wolf has retreated to a far corner

he is standing stiff-legged
his mane on end
head lowered to fight
eyes fixed on the human

the unsteady drunken man pulls the trigger

the roar so sudden so loud
a violent shot of pain explodes in their heads

Wolf jumps
not understanding what has happened

he has never been shot at before

missed

smoke in the air
the garage suddenly feels like a much smaller space

yuh missed him loser

the Alpha male grabs the gun from his friend's hand

I'll show yuh how this is done

unexpectedly

from across the street

the female comes hurrying up the driveway with the two sons

what's going on?

I was havin' coffee over at Betty's and heard this loud noise

get out of the way

we captured a wolf in the garage

the older boy asks

c'n we see'm Dad?

sure

take a look

I don't want them looking

you're trying to kill it

not an "it"

a big male

we'll have braggin' rights at the legion tuhnight!

before she can stop them
both boys have their heads at the hole

the older boy pulls back
grins
I wanna see yuh shoot'm Dad

the younger boy remains staring at the impressive wild creature

something strange happens

Wolf is staring into the boy's eyes
the boy thinks *everything else is wolf*
but the eyes are human

the wife screams
if you shoot that animal
I'll have the conservation officer after you!

she roughly grabs the boys' hands
and drags them into the house

the dinted aluminum door rattles shut

buddy

we're goin' home

don' wanna be in the middle of this

his friends depart across the snowy lawn

alone now

he hesitates

sticks his arm in with the gun

then his head

Wolf smells the chemical of fear in the man's sweat

runs at the door with great force

the man pulls back in panic

– a tremendous crash –

four paws and Wolf's one hundred and seventy-five pounds hit the door

break the old wooden door loose from its hinges

Wolf scrambles

claws scratching fiercely over the wood of the door

the man underneath landing hard on his back hollering wildly panic-stricken

the man accidentally fires the gun

the bullet disappearing along the ground under the snow

the three in the house rushing out the side door

get a brief thrilling glimpse

across their backyard

Wolf

running at top speed

a grey giant

stretched out to full length

legs reaching pulling reaching pulling ground under him

tail lying flat out

coursing through the flying snow

disappearing into the white spruce at the edge of their property

* * *

in five minutes Wolf is deep into the snowbound bush

trotting at a steady pace

cutting along a ridge thick with cedars

he stops and studies in fine detail

the plumage of a whiskey jack pecking on a low branch

looking past the bird

to the middle of a sun-filled open pasture

his eyes can only see at that distance in blurry outline

a form he has grown to know well

a grey-brown stag

like a statue

then the stag begins to move off

like a lord

stiff-legged

arched neck

head held high

Wolf bursts forward

lunges down the hillside dodging trees and bushes

into the field

unaware of Wolf powering forward in full stride behind him

the stag walks toward a small herd of dark-red Herefords

beyond the stone fence in the next field

where he knows there will be hay bales for feeding

a quick snap of legs

over the fence in a graceful arc

he steps carefully

approaching the feeding cows who lift their heads

turn their curly white faces to recognize him

and unconcerned continue lazily grinding their jaws from side to side

by now Wolf is hitting the top of the stone fence

seeing the dreaded enemy

the Herefords suddenly start up

clop away through the snow in their clumsy style

hooves clunking on the frozen ground

the stag

sensing danger

turns to see the grey wolf closing in fast

flips up his foot-long white tail

runs for his life

the Herefords are now charging as quickly as they can

toward their safe home

the barn

Wolf veers to his left to chase the stag lunging up the hillside

at the bottom of the hill

in the corner of his eye

Wolf notices he has been joined in the chase

by an animal almost as tall as himself

this animal is a muscular black-and-white hound

running hard

the hound has caught up

and is now a partner in the chase

as they charge up the high hill

along the windswept bare ridge on the hilltop

the stag increases his lead

his pursuers unable to run at thirty miles per hour for very long

into the heavy bush in the deep crusted snow
in the next few minutes
the stag is working very hard
his sharp hooves cutting through the crust
struggling up to his belly at times in the snow
Wolf and the hound using their large paws like snowshoes
running on the snow's surface

in half an hour they gain on their prey

the stag's shins are bloody

this is a young healthy buck
so their strategy is to run him as best they can
till he is exhausted

Wolf is built for running
with a strong narrow chest and long legs close together
and the hound is a professional hunting dog
specializing in deer

in his youth Wolf was used to hunting with his brother
so he accepts the hound called Le Grand Chien Français

the stag is beginning to tire

blood in his tracks

atop a hill in some white pines
he stops to rest
to gather himself
Wolf and Le Grand are slowly stalking him up the incline

the stag looks down at them with large wet brown eyes
frightened but defiant

as they draw near
he moves off slowly at first
but as they mount the hilltop
he lunges down the other side
unluckily sinks into a large snowdrift up to his belly

they close on him
Wolf risks biting at the hind legs trying to cut the tendons
the stag's back legs kicking dangerously

a broken jaw would mean the end of the hunt

starvation and death in the coming days

Le Grand is circling

attacks the head

a tremendous surge of power

the stag lurches free of the snowdrift

gallops down the hill floundering in the deep snow

Wolf has caught no scent of illness or infection

this will be a hard kill

the stag hits a stretch of river

slipping and skidding on bare spots

using up a lot of energy

but stays on the ice where the wind has blown the snow clear

he is wearing down

Wolf and Le Grand have settled into a comfortable determined lope they could run like this all day

the stag disappears around a bend
out of sight behind a jutting granite riverbank

Wolf and Le Grand come around it

surprise

the stag is standing still

head down

exhausted

they approach him carefully
he swings round and round turning kicking
thrusting at them with his head
catching Le Grand tossing him ten feet back

uninjured because the stag has not yet grown antlers

Le Grand again circles to the head

courageous and ferocious he continues attacking

gets thrown once more

at that precise moment Wolf attacks the rump

his large strong canines breaking through the thick hide

drawing blood

the stag bawls out his pain

kicking

swinging his head

but less fiercely now

Wolf hits the rump again

his one hundred and seventy-five pounds buckling the stag's back legs

Le Grand has caught the nose

holding on determinedly

shaking it violently

the stag giving in

all four legs collapse

Wolf attacks the throat

rips at it

clamps down

holds firm

the stag on his side now

held motionless by his strong attackers

blood in his lungs

in a few moments choking on his own blood

the last weak stirring of the legs

then all movement ceases

Le Grand and Wolf stand back panting

tongues lolling out of their mouths

a bright harsh noon sun shines on the sad still bloody scene

the farmer

a dog fancier

out his kitchen window had seen the chase begin

and would brag later that his powerful hound

Le Grand Chien Français

made the kill a sure thing

his breathing quiet
and his strength returned
Wolf rips open the belly
and feeds on the liver
his favourite organ

there is no fight for the carcass
as there might be in a wolf pack

Le Grand Chien Français has done his job
he will eat at home on the farm

he trots off not looking back
disappears quickly into the bush

Wolf eats his fill from the entrails
for he may not eat again for many days hunting alone
he walks away
abandoning the carcass to wolverines coyotes or other wolves
he continues on the river ice
till he finds a cave under an overhanging rock at the shoreline

he pees at the entrance and enters the cave
lies down in the darkness deep inside
his tail curled over his face
his warm breath keeping his nose from freezing
and sleeps a safe and contented sleep

* * *

Wolf awakens at dawn
stands up and stretches

first he bows his head and front legs
then his stomach and back legs

an unpleasant but familiar scent greets him

on a sleeping mat of dried leaves in a corner
he discovers a surprise companion curled up asleep

a cat-sized animal
covered with silky black fur decorated with startling splashes of white
two white stripes running along its back
a white-tipped bushy tail

a white cap on its head

and a thin white line running down the middle of its face

under the tail a small brown rubbery nose raises up

beady dark wet eyes open

and showing no fear or panic close again

Wolf does not realize

this stinking polecat has just returned from scavenging

on the stag carcass during the night

and having shared dens with foxes and raccoons many times

hasn't hesitated sharing with a wolf

Wolf remembers this cocky creature from his youth

when inexperienced and foolish

he was sprayed and temporarily blinded

unaware his companion is a solitary male

Wolf departs quickly

to avoid meeting the stinky family that might show up

a great horned owl

the striped skunk's deadliest enemy

could swoop down unseen out of the sky

and kill this creature when he leaves the cave

but for now he is safe

bad memories will keep Wolf at bay

he heads down the frozen river to the kill site

to see if there is anything left to eat

after the scavengers have feasted

* * *

five miles upriver

at the top of a white pine eighty-five feet high

a terrible squawking is going on

under branches that provide good cover

in a triple crotch that gives firm support

four black nestlings stretch their gaping beaks

out over the rim of a giant wicker basket

- a nest three feet by three feet and six inches deep

they are as safe as they could possibly be

and although the late April wind is very cold

they are warm in the nest lined with the white belly fur of a deer

but they are hungry

they are *always* hungry

high in the clear blue sky above

strange sounds

RRONK RRONK

KORRP KORRP

TOC TOC TOC

an enormous creature

calling out

descends

on wings spanning four feet

completely black

with a touch of blue glistening down its back feathers

twisting and rolling out of control

sure for disaster

RRONK . . . RRONK . . .

tips of the large rough wing feathers spread wide like ghastly fingers

now twisting into several somersaults

KORRP . . . KORRP . . .

falling dangerously close to the helpless nestlings
he suddenly rights himself

just having a little fun

he lands with skill on one of the branches supporting the nest

from his heavy curved beak he spits up meat
into each starving squalling red throat
his long wedge-shaped tail dipping back and forth for balance

this bird
holds back some meat in his throat for his smaller mate
the female taking a break nearby
who now swoops in for a landing and her share

she eats and returns to her babysitting in the nest

her male partner
a great black northern raven
jumps into the sky from the edge of the nest
soaring downward on outstretched wings
heads back to the stag carcass on the frozen river

loping along the ice
Wolf hears the throaty *RRONK RRONK*
looks skyward to spy Raven twirling down in the blue
and Wolf increases his speed
knowing full well what the presence of Raven means

coming in sight of the blood-red carcass surrounded by wolf tracks
Wolf can see that little remains of the stag
- it has been a long hard winter –
some of the animals are near starving

several grey jays are flitting about
three young ravens jumping up and down
their wings lifted high flapping
fighting for position
but carefully avoiding an ill-tempered thirty-pound wolverine

the powerful vicious "skunk bear"
also called "evil spirit" by the anishinabeg
is busy cracking rib bones with his strong jaws
to get at meat and marrow

letting loose a frightening *KORRP KORRP*
Raven dives low over the group

the young ravens fly off a little way
landing in a scrawny tamarack

the jays remain at a distance

the wolverine only looks up a moment from his feeding
holding a leg bone down with the long curled claws of his front paws

Raven dive-bombs a second time
the wolverine turns to face the bird
and bares his teeth
raises the hair on its back
lifts its tail

Raven in passing hears a low blood-curdling growl

but is still unable to scare the fierce creature away

Wolf comes charging up
teeth bared
sees wolverine swinging around to face him

Wolf runs right over top of the wolverine
sends him sprawling

gaining his feet the wolverine decides to scuttle off
rather than fight this powerhouse enemy

Wolf watches his opponent scramble up the snowbank
then begins to pick the bones for what scraps of meat remain
as Raven lands opposite him

setting his head on one side and then the other
Raven looks at Wolf with slowly blinking eyes
begins picking at the bones with his heavy down-curved black beak

Wolf makes no move toward Raven

they feed in peace

over his lifetime Wolf has been directed to a prey or a carcass

many times by the familiar hoarse squawking of a raven

and they have been partners in feeding

Wolf first and Raven second

this time

the leftovers are so few that both creatures are still hungry

Wolf decides to continue upriver to hunt

Raven follows

soaring high

swooping low

Raven makes playful close passes over Wolf

Wolf playfully making half-hearted runs at Raven

the weary travellers are on the river all morning

these two rugged creatures do not go south in winter

they tough it out

they spit in the face of winter

in this harsh life with its many dangers

Wolf may only live ten years

perhaps bleeding to death from a serious wound

or starving

unable to eat

his jaw broken by a kick from a moose or a deer

or dying from rabies or heartworm or mange

Raven

the most intelligent of birds

will likely live to be thirty or maybe forty

feeding on the dead

not a predator risking all to bring down the ungulates

moose deer elk

as Wolf will try to do

Wolf scratches a hollow in a snowdrift

curls up in his usual position

falls asleep

as he sleeps

snowfall covers him completely

protects him from the cold sunless afternoon

in the dimming light of early evening

he awakens

stands up and shakes off the snow

without knowing it he frightens a lynx passing in the trees behind him

who bounds away silently on its ridiculously long back feet

Wolf searches the sky

Raven is gone

* * *

though it is late April

the long seven-month winter is hanging on

The Great Northern Forest

is two big things

fire and ice

right now it's ice

and Wolf travels steadily all day on the river

and the large lake it joins

tracks of the snowshoe hare are few

in this year of a low birth cycle

he has not eaten since morning

and with dusk coming on

he enters the bush hoping to surprise a rabbit

a mole

or even a mouse

anything to quiet the hunger in his belly

in the bushes and evergreens and bare white birch

he does smell out a few mice under the snow

dig them up for a snack

high above him out of sight

as he passes along the bottom of an overhanging outcrop

a large bull moose

only buds of antlers beginning to show on his knobby head

is hunkered down in a drift

tired at the end of the day and saving energy

Wolf might not be able to bring down this animal anyway

without a pack to help him

a pair of fun-loving chickadees

buzz back and forth past Wolf's head

like tiny black-and-white helicopters

then disappear into the handsome tapering spire of a balsam fir

leaving only their saucy *dee dee dee* ringing in the frigid air

Wolf finally finds an old den of a black bear

under the large roots of a giant white spruce

before he settles in for the night

standing at the entrance to the den

he lifts his head and sends out a long forlorn howl

silence

he howls again

silence

then

a high wild chorus begins

five voices

wavering warbling

more or less together

following one another

soon breaking off into crazy overlapping solos

a pack of wolves

strangers to him

somewhere out there in the fading light

they carry on for a while

having a great deal of fun

and when they stop

although he does not recognize any voices

he is less lonely

* * *

in early May

after eleven days and nights on linked rivers and lakes

sleeping rarely

surviving on moles and mice

and one snowshoe hare

in grey dusk Wolf holes up in an abandoned wolf den

in use for over a hundred years

exhausted

falls asleep

* * *

in the morning light
he again travels by river
stays near shore
careful not to fall through the bare thinning ice
now weakened by days of warm afternoon sunshine

by noon
skirting a small northern Ontario Ojibway village called Nakina
he stops on a hilltop to rest

he studies the landscape carefully
as wolves often do
because they don't see well at a distance

he sees at the dump outside of the village the shapes of gulls
and by their movements and noisy squawking
understands they are feeding on something good

when Wolf arrives he learns the something good is a dog carcass
and joins in the feeding
although little meat is left

having lost weight and feeling weak
he continues his journey slowly north along a logging road
and picks up the trail of a wolf pack
cuts into the bush
the tracks soon circling around a deer yard
a grove of black spruce with the snow inside packed down
where deer have been resting and gathering together for safety

Wolf retreats to the trees a little way off to watch and wait
not realizing other predators are also hidden

waiting

suddenly
that roaring beast noise explodes in his ears
only this time there are two beasts
smaller beasts
with high-pitched voices
coming straight at him with lightning speed
around the edge of the deer yard

Wolf can see each has a human riding on its back
but he doesn't know the humans have handguns in their parkas
and they are wolfers
men who on weekends enjoy running down and killing wolves
selling the hides to pay for beer and gasoline
sometimes seventy-five bucks for one wolf pelt

instantly Wolf heads into the deep bush to shake his pursuers
running hard
fearful of the strange enemy
he snakes his way through the thickest bushes and trees

the beasts follow but fall back
twisting and diving over drifts
landing with a bang
gunning forward
slowing down around big trees or bare ground
making sounds Wolf thinks are angry screams

for long minutes Wolf runs
hearing the terrifying whine and growl behind him

he is losing strength and slowing down

no longer able to run at top speed

the wolfers on their snow machines are enjoying themselves
laughing and shouting and pointing
starting to gain on Wolf as he tires

Wolf scrambles around an outcrop and onto a river
heads for the windblown bare spots where the running will be easier

he is halfway to the other side as the wolfers reach the river

now that they can see Wolf ahead
and don't have to search for tracks to follow
they speed up
the front end of their machines bouncing up
barely touching the surface at times
then hammering down on the ice

the lead machine is powerful
makes a wide circle and cuts Wolf off before he can reach shore
the other coming up behind to prevent Wolf from turning back

there will be no sportsmanship

no marksmanship

only running Wolf till he is totally exhausted and can run no more

then putting a handgun to his head and killing him

by now

running along the shoreline

Wolf is without hope

somehow he gives one last burst

cuts behind the lead snowmobile

and gains the shore

at that spot a large creek has been draining spring runoff for days

into the river under the ice

making a sharp turn

following Wolf to the shoreline

the big heavy machine with a two-hundred-pound man on it

breaks through the ice worn away underneath by the creek's flow

and sinks out of sight

the panicked gasping man surfaces
just his head above the bone-freezing water
treading his arms wildly

the second driver slows down
veers off from the mouth of the creek
drives ashore where the ice is thicker
and runs back along the bank
stopping to aid his pal

Wolf notices the beasts are no longer in pursuit
keeps on at the best pace he can manage for a few minutes
till he stops to listen and be sure he is now safe

panting
his sides heaving
his tongue hanging out the side of his mouth
for a short time he listens carefully
watches the woods with that intense wolf stare

he is sure now

no more beasts

using what strength remains he walks till dusk

at last denning up under a huge fallen spruce trunk

where he will remain unmoving till dawn

* * *

in his journey

Wolf has made a big circle south and back north toward his home

travelling about five hundred miles in the last month

crossing many worn trails

and the scent-marked territories of many wolf packs

who would have tried to run him down and kill him as an intruder

if they had discovered him

he comes across the body of a lone female wolf

freshly killed by a pack for trespassing

he stops to look

and check the scent of her attackers

left by the scent glands in their paws

then carries on

later he is walking along the shoreline of Winisk Lake

careful of thin ice

stopping to watch the top of a black spruce

where a bald eagle takes off

the famous strong downturned yellow beak of the kingly white head

the white tail on the large black body

flapping his broad wings spanning seven feet

in big slow powerful strokes

flying back farther into the bush

wary of Wolf

at noon he comes upon tracks and scat of three adult wolves

follows them into the bush for several miles

till he hears the yipping of two pups

stops to listen

approaches slowly a clearing by a small stream

a rendezvous spot

where the five-month-old pups have been left to play and sleep

while the three adults have gone hunting

he waits

hidden in some tamarack

soon to see the Alpha female arrive

the pups running to her

licking her muzzle to make her throw up meat she has brought them

suddenly a loud thrashing fills Wolf's ears

two attacking males pound his back with startling heavy impact

a large black wolf and a smaller white one

young and strong and quick

loud snarling the click of large canine teeth

a vicious flurry of fur bloodcurdling cries brute force

he is down on his back

the smell of blood

his attackers ripping at stomach head legs

the bigger of the two trying to pierce his throat and finish him off

Wolf with a surprising thrust rolls over

throwing them off

gains his feet

now his superior weight and strength backs them up

he grabs the smaller by the muzzle shakes him ferociously

hurling him aside and runs at the bigger with a savage charge

knocking him on his back

standing on his chest

powerful fangs inches from the exposed throat

under the great weight and power

the young wolf only lightly pressing his paws against Wolf's chest

submits

his younger brother runs off into the bush

Wolf gets off the black wolf

stands close facing him

staring directly into the rusty-orange eyes

establishing control

the young wolf does not move

he is not a coward

but he knows he is beaten

Wolf turns away

runs to the female

she smiles a vicious smile

growling fiercely

guarding the pups cowering behind her

Wolf has no wish to harm her or the pups

he walks up to her slowly

carefully

lowers his head and tail

waits for calm and silence

after long moments of quiet

Wolf draws near

licks her muzzle

she relaxes

the two pups approach

gangly and fuzzy-haired with big feet stumbling over one another

old enough that their milk teeth have been replaced by adult teeth

and their ears are no longer folded down

ears pricked up and alert

they begin to maul Wolf

pulling his tail

biting his legs

jumping up and sliding off his tall back

whining and whimpering

licking his muzzle hoping for food

Wolf is very patient

as all adult wolves are with pups

he gently knocks them down and pushes them about with his nose

holds them down in turn under one large front paw

play-bites them

holding their muzzles in his

the Alpha female steps in

and leads her pups away

heading back toward their den

Wolf follows at a distance

minutes later at the entrance to the den
the pups dive in chasing each other

Mother sits at the entrance

Wolf lies down some yards away

the early evening passes

at dusk
Mother has disappeared inside for the night

Wolf finds a quiet refuge under the lower limbs of a small black spruce

* * *

awakening in the morning light
Wolf hears the pups making a fuss inside

Mother appears
leading them back to the rendezvous spot
where they will sport and explore and wait for breakfast or lunch
or whatever may happen

Wolf follows at some distance
soon joining the pups
and putting up with their nonsense all morning
until tired of being mauled and jumped on
he follows Mother's scent to the lake to check on her hunting

at the lake's edge
he can only dimly make out a blurry speck
moving toward him over the dangerous grey ice
skirting open water

he waits calmly as the shape gets larger and larger
till he recognizes Mother
and the long ears and legs of a snowshoe hare flopping in her jaws

she makes no sign of acceptance
trots by him onto the trail to the rendezvous spot

arriving she is greeted by wild yipping
as the two crazy pups charge out of their hiding places
and assault her for food

behind them appears the big black young male
standing still and waiting for permission at the edge of the clearing

because he has not been chased off
he comes along at a polite distance
as the others head back to the den

in the den
Mother rips the hare apart and the pups feed greedily

she saves a small portion for herself

the adult males bed down for the night
a respectful distance apart

* * *

in the next few weeks
this pattern repeats itself over and over

the only change is that Wolf
is now the first Beta
and regularly joins Mother hunting each day

and the black male in the role of the second Beta male
escorts the pups on the hunt
or guards them if they are left behind

late afternoons or early evenings
Wolf and Mother bring home small game
ptarmigan vole coyote partridge
and the order of eating
according to wolf law
is followed

Mother the Alpha eats first
then Wolf
then Black
who stands aside watching patiently
his rusty-orange eyes alert for his turn
the pups eat last

one day
at the beginning of the second month of the new family
travelling along the rocky shore
because the ice is gone from Winisk Lake
Wolf and Mother are following the tracks of an arctic fox
when Wolf's peripheral vision glimpses a passing shadow in the bush

Mother seeing the direction of his glance
begins to watch the bush also as they follow the fox tracks
– from time to time a quick flash of grey a shadow a twig snapping –
but they never quite get a clear enough look
to see who is stalking them

in a small gully they see a white arctic fox
still in his winter coat
feeding on a cache of deer meat he has stolen from a recent kill site

in the rustle of busily covering up his cache with twigs and rocks
he does not hear his enemies approach

Wolf pounces quickly from behind
snaps the tiny neck cleanly

a quick merciful killing

the pair head back home
still aware of being followed
along the gravel shore no longer covered with snow
they stop
and hear the gravel rattle a bit as their pursuer stops behind them

as they cut into the bush heading for their den
Mother continues on when Wolf circles back

coming up behind
passing over the rendezvous spot
well-tramped down so quiet movement is possible
Wolf spies the stalker ten yards ahead
slipping along unaware

Wolf quickly closes the gap
is surprised

the stalker is a male wolf

he stops short
turning to face up to his danger
a lost ragged wolf
with haunted eyes
gaping jaws
ribs showing
fur matted
a helpless starving wolf
the smaller white brother who fled in the fight at the rendezvous spot

Wolf approaches close

sniffing around the scent gland at the base of his tail

recognizes the young creature

and passes by

allowing the lost pack member to come along unharmed

at the den

the small arctic fox provides a mere morsel to each pack member

the youngest brother feeding last

too little food to do him any good

they all bed down for the night hungry

White lying with Wolf and Black at the entrance

* * *

in the morning the pack enters a new stage in its life

at six months

the pups have been going along on the hunt from time to time

but now they are ready to actually learn the skills

and participate in the kill

they have inborn instinct
but without training they will never be hunters
never master the many techniques and strategies of the hunt

they go wild when they pass the rendezvous spot

they gallop and bark
nipping and chasing one another
making far too much noise

finally
before reaching the beach
Wolf and Mother stop short

stand still long enough staring at the two rapscallions
that they get the message

be quiet

at the same moment
left behind
too weak to be of any use
White has limped into the den to lie down
and sleep away the day

along the rocky beach of Winisk Lake
the pack finds no game
but enjoys the awakening morning

the pups have been well behaved and have not tired yet

at noon when the sun is hottest
they all stop to drink at a stream
and take cover in the bush for a nap

in The Great Northern Forest the world is coming alive

the bald eagle
circling high in the blue sky
feels the strong warmth of the late spring sun
sees many things far below him

pussy willows budding in the shallow creeks

splashing river otters slipping smoothly through the water like snakes
happily fishing and playing tag

awkward black bear cubs

still round and fuzzy-haired

exploring stumbling wrestling rolling with great pleasure

mother bear nearby keeping a watchful eye

beaver kits with small blunt faces and greasy wet brown fur

at the edges of rivers nibbling saplings in the still cold waters

and high in the northern sky

white snow geese and Canada geese winging their way to summer nesting

he can see too

the pack working deeper and deeper into the bush

in the afternoon they come upon a Cree tent in a clearing by a lake

hearing the happy teasing chatter of the Cree family inside

plucking feathers from geese they have shot and cooking the meat

astam (come inside)

eat   eat

the mother is calling the children chasing each other through the camp

come in now

smelling the fire

and the delicious goose meat and onions and baked beans

the wolves will check for leftovers on the return journey later

after the anishinabeg have gone

their only chance for a kill goes unnoticed

left alone for hours by her mother

a small defenseless fawn

a singleton

luckily at this age giving off no scent

lies invisible and still

her spots blending into the underbrush

the pack walks right by her hiding place

and continues on

scattered under the trees they take a late afternoon nap

then the long journey home begins

passing the Cree goose camp

they see the anishinabeg enjoying supper

staying in camp for another day

the pack passes on

arriving back at their den after dark with no food for White

* * *

the next morning

a morning in late July

Mother awakens the pups in the den

a long trek north along the Winisk River will begin today

following a woodland caribou herd on its way to summer territory

on the west coast of Hudson Bay

White emerges from the den

shaky and feeble

of all the pack he has been hurt the most from lack of food

a scarcity of prey in the area means the wolves have no choice

they must follow the caribou

so

all summer

neither the wolves nor the caribou will keep a home territory they trot for the last time along the cool well-worn trail

and past the old rendezvous spot

in the fresh piney scent brought alive by overnight showers

then on to the rocky beach

where the day is already heating up

high humidity

high winds

the constant sun all morning

later creates an afternoon storm

after the quick shower

Wolf leads the pack off the river inland to the cool wet windless bush

moving quickly to avoid the swarms of blackflies

hours later

with the ability to smell caribou miles away in the clear still air

the adults pick up the scent

a herd of woodland caribou

in celebration

the wolves stage a brief crazy rally

yipping and chasing each other

dodging in and around the trees

the adults joining in the fun

for the first time Mother and Black paw at Wolf in a teasing way

and play a favourite game

jump out of hiding and surprise him

the rally ends with a great joyful howling session

their voices as usual soaring and dipping and wavering and overlapping

a wild haunting discord

the pups love the chance to practise their weak howls

throwing back their short blunt fuzzy muzzles

and concentrating hard

very seriously shooting sound straight up into the sky

too worked up and out of control

they may scare off game by rushing forward noisily

but they are allowed their fun

White does not join in
but his spirits seem improved

all afternoon Wolf and Black lead the pack through mature forests
around open bogs and low-lying wetlands and across soggy meadows
the caribou always ahead out of sight somewhere

by now calmed down and accompanied by Mother
the pups are still keen and full of energy
especially the larger of the two
thrusting forward through the grasses and shrubs
her beautiful tawny coat shining in the open sunlit meadows

her slightly smaller silver-grey brother is handsome too
slipping along behind her

White has dropped far back
they come across a garbage-strewn fishing camp with rotting cabins
a sagging clothesline rusty soup cans
plastic shopping bags tangled in bushes
a broken-down snowmobile
empty beer and liquor bottles
old magazines broken glass abandoned clothing

to the wolves the human scent inside the cabins is disturbing

no food left behind

continuing along the Winisk River
Wolf notices within a few miles the caribou scent grows stronger

he has observed along the way the signs of a small herd
stopping to feed on willow leaves sedges grasses mushrooms

he expects to find in this small herd at least two or three calves
born in late May or early June
easy pickings in the hunt

finally
Wolf catches a glimpse

the rich dark brown rump of a large four-hundred-pound bull
and a flash of white neck and chest

Black and Wolf and Mother fan out a bit
immediately break into a wild surprise run
to startle the herd and chase it
testing for likely prey

suddenly in all directions

flashes of rich brown and dazzling white appear through the green

the caribou are mad with fear

there is a great bashing and crashing through the boreal forest

the snapping of twigs the swish of branches

the bawling snorting farting hoof-thumping gasping flight

the steel-eyed wolves run at a controlled hard-driving pace

watching carefully to select a possible victim

the herd breaking apart and hard to see in the forest

the pups Tawny and Silver

at first making a halting approach to the chase

stop

slightly confused

watch in amazement

then can't keep up

White is nowhere in sight

in time Wolf selects an old bull

who is creaky with arthritis and slow and slightly lame

but

for now

after this short burst at top speed

about thirty miles an hour for a few minutes through the rough bush

they stop running hard

they lope along in their relaxed rocking-horse style

following the scent of the herd

catching their breath

allowing the herd to pull ahead

darkness is coming on

and although their night vision is excellent

the tired wolves will wait to make an organized assault later

leaving White far behind

into the night the pack follows the caribou slowly through the bush

making no noise

eventually lying down to sleep

knowing full well they can easily trace the scent

and catch up to the herd later

* * *

in the morning White drags himself into their midst
as the pack members are awakening

Tawny and Silver rush to him
but he has no energy to roughhouse

Wolf steps in and ushers the playful pups away

White lies down on his side and remains there as the pack moves off

midmorning
following scent
a rustle tells Wolf that caribou are near

the first caribou encountered is not the old bull
but the largest strongest young bull
the leader
four hundred pounds of power
xalibu
"the one who paws" in the Mi'kmaq language
he is pawing for lichens
then suddenly aware of the wolves
rears up on his hind legs

using scent glands at the base of his ankles
to deposit danger scent to alert the others

the rest of the herd has spread out enough to be out of sight
but Wolf can hear them crashing through the bush in flight

this powerful bull will have to be their prey
if they wish to be sure of eating today

a lightning missile shooting forward
Wolf charges the head fiercely
Black and Mother circling the animal's flanks
looking for an opportunity to bite into the muscle of a back leg
or jump onto the back and bite into the rump to help disable the bull

Wolf is hanging on the hide under the strong neck

in a rush of panic and adrenalin
the powerful bull shakes Wolf in mid air like a rag doll

Wolf lets go

the wolves circle and circle looking for openings

the bull circling also
hoping to deal a death blow with his hooves
still heavy and thick from winter growth

he lunges at them
thrusting his short amber antlers
not grown large enough yet to be dangerous weapons

Black hits the side of the neck and rips a bloody gash in the flesh
an ugly flap of hide dangling
the bull roaring like a nightmare monster

Wolf and Mother immediately jump with full force on the back
bringing the bull to his knees

Black grabs the muzzle and hangs on
despite the bull regaining his feet and lunging forward

Wolf joins Black
attacking the throat again
and the combined weight of the two males brings the bull down
face first into the ground

Mother too joins the attack upon the head

the bull is in real trouble now
the wolves sense their advantage and go with it
exerting every bit of jaw force they can manage

viciously Wolf changes his grip
smothering the animal's muzzle and nose in killer jaws
jaws clamped with fifteen hundred pounds of bone-crushing pressure
preventing the caribou from breathing

the young bull thrashes his legs
shakes his head in terror unable to breathe
but nothing will stop these wolves now
they have gone far too long without food
they are near to starving and death themselves
they will not be beaten here
and within short minutes
the unfortunate bull has passed out from lack of oxygen
his lungs full of his own wild blood

he slumps into stillness
the four desperate animals locked together on the leafy forest floor
in a gruesome sculpture of death

Mother is the first to move

she is trapped under the bull's neck
and wriggles herself loose
stands up
giving herself a shake

Wolf and Black let loose their grip on the neck and muzzle

the two males stand slowly and move back
panting
tongues hanging out
still full of adrenalin
letting their fear drain away

finally the pups come frightened out of hiding in the nearby tamarack

they are frightened of their own family members
the terrible force and violence they saw turned loose
in the bloody death scene

the pups approach quietly whimpering
licking the muzzles of Wolf and Mother and Black

composing himself

Wolf rips open the belly of the carcass

pulling the hide back

Mother and Wolf begin feeding first

savouring the liver

always a favourite organ

Black joins in feeding on the warm entrails

then Tawny and Silver join the feast

these starving animals fill their bulging bellies

the adults with as much as twenty pounds of meat each

when they are satisfied

they move off a short way into the nearby grove of tamarack

and sleep away a good part of the afternoon

* * *

in late afternoon

the pack is retracing its journey from earlier in the day

looking to find White

they find him at dusk in an abandoned black bear den

Tawny and Silver rush to him as usual for play
sniff him all over
but Wolf knows

White is dead

as wolves do
each adult in turn approaches
and lies down beside the thin ragged creature to mourn
Tawny and Silver
at first stand back
then copy the adult behaviour
whining and pawing at their brother

*

later travelling through the dark
using their excellent night vision
the pack returns to the caribou kill site

they chase away a red fox and a murder of crows

and gorge themselves once again

* * *

in the morning
the pack is assembled back at the entrance to the bear den
each family member in turn entering to lie with the lost companion

if they were in their home territory
they might continue mourning for days in this manner
but now their survival depends on tracking the caribou
so they leave the lost one
and make their way toward Hudson Bay
through The Great Northern Forest

on this the second day of their journey up the Winisk River
the wolves are strong and energetic

a light shower only serves to refresh them in the warm afternoon

they see ahead up the rocky shore a campsite
abandoned that morning by a couple of canoeists
skirt it
always shy of humans

at that very moment
fifteen miles along the Winisk
a bright-red seventeen-foot Old Town Tripper canoe
is tipped on its side onshore

in its shade the young couple
collapsed together asleep on a rocky outcrop
their Tilley hats pulled over their faces
too tired after half a day's paddling to eat their shore lunch

behind the couple's camp in a marshy creek
Tawny and Silver curiously sniff a painted turtle
who plops into the water and slides out of sight
toward the creek bottom

farther along the creek
Tawny and Silver abandon themselves to their natural playfulness
not shy of water like some other predators
built to run
long skinny legs
muscular chests
they open up and fly through the cool shallows
splashing and yipping

chasing each other in wide skidding arcs

water flying around them

slender bodies under the dripping wet fur

mouths open in happy smiles

ears erect

wet faces

red tongues

they feel joy of being young and full of spirit

clear eyes alert to everything

soon they notice

the adults have disappeared farther into the bush

looking for scent of caribou or moose

the pups hastily catch up following the familiar scent

travelling in a huge sweep back to the Winisk

by evening when they find themselves in a quiet marshy bay

luck smiles on them

a moose calf

alone

separated from his mother

without a second of hesitation Black runs the shore at speed
from behind tackles the alerted helpless calf splashing for shore
snaps its neck

the rest of the pack arrives quickly
Black drags the male calf ashore

muzzles stained red with blood
jaws twice as strong as a German shepherd's crunch the bones
consume bone and marrow and meat

unseen just back from shore in some black spruce
the moose cow is standing motionless
staring
unable to do anything

when the wolves finished feeding on her calf
and trotted up the shore out of sight
the cow approaches nervously
sniffs at the remains
then quietly disappears back into the bush

seeking to cross the Winisk
the pack comes upon rapids too dangerous for the pups to swim

Wolf decides they will take refuge on an island
surrounded by a dry rock garden of huge round boulders
an area where the river has dried up

the adults leap lightly from boulder to boulder
but Tawny and Silver
not so skilled and sure-footed
scramble up and over and at times slide down between the boulders
yelping scratching and falling

on the island and feeling secure
each wolf chooses a spot to bed down in the willows
and lying contented in the growing dusk
they watch five large osprey fly out of the piney uplands
hovering over the rapids on wings spanning five or six feet

one huge bird circling thirty metres above the water
suddenly dives with its wings half closed
and open claws stretched forward
plunges into the water in a great spray
disappears below the surface

he emerges in seconds with a two-foot-long northern pike

flies into the bush carrying its catch headfirst

followed by its mate

the other three osprey remain

hovering

cheeep . . . cheeep . . . cheeep

as the light fades

* * *

day three on the long journey

begins with two common golden-eye ducks

squawking in the trees above the sleeping pack

the wolves all arise and stretch and head for the river

in the quiet morning

the river water is cool and refreshing running down their throats

the upper Winisk
is far too fast-flowing for Tawny and Silver to swim across
so the pack heads along the grey outcrop of the rocky shore
to find the caribou herd again

Tawny and Silver have lost the blue eyes they were born with
and now with intense yellow eyes
carefully watch the adults and imitate and learn

inland looking for scent

shaking blackflies off their faces

walking quietly on the comfort of dry sphagnum moss

skirting slow-thawing bogs

they work their way along wet muddy trails
their noses alive to the scents and tracks left by many creatures

at a brief rest stop
in a clearing of golden sunlight
a dragonfly lands on Silver's nose

Tawny swats at it
cuffing her brother in the face

as the unharmed insect whizzes away
Silver tackles his sister
the pair roll in the dry grass

a brief dusty wrestling match

Tawny wins
as she always does
standing over her brother baring her teeth
asserting her superiority

early in the afternoon they find the herd
make several scrambling runs through the forest without success
but at least Tawny and Silver are now getting the idea
running in a circling pattern trying to help trap their prey

except for some salmon berries
by evening they have not eaten
and pick a spot to sleep
up a creek bank running out of Goose Sounding Lake
under some white birch

across the creek in a high open windswept campsite

under the black spruce there sits a red Old Town Tripper upside down

being used as a table by the two humans

later the wolves watch the humans fish in a quiet spot below the rapids

catch two northern pike in the shallows

bring the cleaned fish back to camp and cook them in a small tin oven

the smells of unfamiliar food drift across the creek

to the quiet wolves under the birches

as darkness falls they watch the flicker of the humans' campfire

and hear their strange angry calls

I hate this trip

the river's so wide we can't sneak up on wildlife

they see us coming

and there's nothing to look at

except these terrible scraggly black spruce

a great sunset last night

it doesn't make up for eight hours of hard paddling into the wind

and those boring black spruce

why did you come then?

it's wilderness canoeing not a visit to a spa

you said it would be romantic

but it's just hard work and blackflies

oh honey

we'll have some good times

you'll see

the male human throws a pail of water on the fire

and they crawl into the tent

and zip up

hours later in the complete black of the northern night

Wolf and Black quietly search the campsite for food

and Wolf carries off a food pack in his strong jaws

a mile away along the Winisk shore

Black and Wolf tear apart the canvas pack

among the packages of dried dinners in foil packets
and plastic bags of oatmeal
they find in large baggies some bacon
which all the wolves devour

in the tearing apart of the food pack
a bottle rolls out and breaks
but the wolves pull back from the strong-smelling liquid
spilling onto the dirt

scotch whiskey

perked up by the meat
Wolf leads his pack away from Goose Sounding Lake
and they travel the shore
the highway of the night for many northern animals

* * *

all morning
in the hazy sky
around the sun
a strange halo

they stop for a drink

as wolves are known to do sometimes
they gaze at the unfamiliar
in this case the dim sun veiled in a halo

later in mid afternoon they are passing the Bearhead Rapids

fascinated by the shallow rushing water
Silver steps into a fast-running chute at the water's edge
gets swept through
and comes flailing and spitting out the other end
dogpaddling fiercely for shore

the others watch him shake himself
with a certain glint in their eyes

wolves love a joke

one day when Wolf was young
his pack was being stalked by a kind but stubborn field naturalist
a wolf expert
sitting as near to them as he dared
his back against a tree trunk

Wolf with a sparkle in his eye approached the gentleman

snatched the ball cap off his head

and ran a few yards

dropping the cap on the ground

standing over it to see what the man would do

the gentleman smiled

waiting some time for the large and dangerous-looking pack

to trot away

before retrieving his Blue Jays cap

by late afternoon on a muddy creek bank

Wolf picks up the scent of the caribou herd again

Tawny and Silver jump around in excitement

the pack follows the scent till darkness

and they wearily bed down

as a heavy rain starts

in the middle of the night

a mysterious and scary prowler of the night woods

famous but seldom seen

three feet long and the swiftest and most agile of the weasel family
who preys on raccoon and sheep and small deer
is suddenly lit up by a fork of lightning

a brief flashbulb glimpse

a sleek dark fisher sliding by under the trees

Silver quickly curls up with Mother and feels much safer

the cracking lightning may start a forest fire
a friend to the jack pine that can only release its seed in such heat
but a terrifying enemy to all the animals of the Great Northern Forest

* * *

happily
at daylight of the fifth day
there is no forest fire near them
although sixty fires are burning that day across Northern Ontario

the downpour continues all that morning
and the pack makes its slow way along the gravel shore single file

the pups are very wet and unhappy

looking very skinny

the soaked fur clinging to their ribs

when Silver nips at the tendon of a back leg to tease her

Tawny snaps at him crankily

about noon

an exciting stretch of white water

the broad and long Tashka Rapids

in high wind and continuing rain

the pack spies a Cree fishing camp

back from the river a bit on a plot of cleared shore

a well-kept camp of three brown wooden cabins set up off the ground

each with a silver aluminum front door and a silver tin roof

they stop and study the camp carefully

to check for humans

then do a sweep through the property

looking sniffing

when they are satisfied the area is safe
they feed on what raspberries are left on the bushes around the camp
a small and not very satisfying lunch

they burrow under the front porch of the middle fishing cabin
and take cover from the rain there

the patient wolves watch the rain all afternoon
flopping on their sides to nap from time to time

at dusk
a moment of interest

through the wall of white rain
nine Canada geese come waddling out of a bay across from the cabins
and over a point of rocky outcrop

too far away for the wolves to sneak up on

they slip calmly into the river and drift by confidently
like royalty
disappearing into the mist with the current of the Winisk
paddling north in the direction of Hudson Bay

as the wolves fall asleep for the night

they hear a mysterious sound

through the wind and rain and rushing rapids

in the trees of the opposite shore

a sound like a chorus of anishinabeg women chanting a hymn

the wolves fall asleep without understanding this sound

* * *

they are awakened the next morning as they usually are

by sounds

this time by loud rain

and two screaming bald eagles

they rouse themselves out of the comfortable dry ground under the cabin

maybe they will face another all-day rain

all scent washed away

no caribou

the pups are not having any fun

but following the example of the adults

they are learning how to keep going and endure

they start along the rocky shore

Wolf

always alert

hears a droning beast noise

and quickly leads his pack into the bush

swooping up out of the south horizon faster than any bird

following the river

a float plane called an Otter

white with a red stripe along its fuselage

and the leading edge of each wing

flying low

it glides over them

carrying aerial hunters holding high-powered rifles

Wolf can see a face stare out a window

looking for something fun to kill

a moose

a caribou

a polar bear

or a wolf

after the Otter disappears over the black spruce horizon

Wolf's ears pick up a deep rumble from farther down the river

a falls or a deep drop-off

they approach Rough Rapids

fast water rushing through chutes

large foaming waves over ledges

dangerous to canoeists

who might overturn and break a leg or arm or lose food packs

a hundred miles from the nearest help

as they pass

each member of the pack glances at the noisy speedy water

*

into the bush in the afternoon

west of the Winisk

the pack visits Kasabonika Lake

bored and tired

Silver is beginning to lag and at times wanders off

missing for minutes at a time

now he catches up

just in time to see the others stopped

watching a loon

clumsy on shore

the loon waddles into the lake where he spends most of his time

and slides under the surface

for long moments he is underwater

the wolves wait

if they could see below

they would observe this aquatic bird

with a near-perfect design one hundred million years old

swooping and swirling around

exploring the geography of his underwater world

which he has memorized

when he finally surfaces

a speck far down the lake

he lets out that famous wailing warble

– to the Cree the cry of a warrior denied entrance to heaven –

they also see along the horizon of the lake

a line of five green canoes proceeding north on a journey

curiosity satisfied

the pack continues along the shore of Lake Kasabonika

Wolf drops back to keep an eye on Silver

Black leading the pack

tail and head held high

Mother and Tawny side by side behind him

after a while

even with Wolf's company

Silver becomes distracted

naturally still immature at six months

he lags behind to sniff at a toad

out of a moment of silence

eight razor-sharp talons hit Silver's side with shocking impact

two claws lock tight

lifting the stunned young wolf into the air

carrying him several yards

before Silver's weight brings the attacking great grey owl back to earth

still locked fiercely onto Silver's back

blood flowing around the talons

the round feathered head bent forward

concentrating on the task at hand

fangs bared

a bloodcurdling growl

Wolf rushes the owl

who sees the other wolves also coming

lets go and lifts off on his big powerful noiseless wings

seven thousand soft feathers designed perfectly for silent flight

not one of the wolves heard the diving great grey

now Silver is licking feverishly at the wounds on his back
as the others surround him
whining
sniffing at him

atop a nearby white birch
sits the dusky grey-striped body nearly three feet long
the round head not rotating 300 degrees as usual looking for prey
but pointed directly at the wolves

like a satellite dish his lined facial disc captures every sound
picks up acutely even the tiniest noise of the wolves in their distress
his round yellow eyes blinking slowly
very interested
the curved scalpel-sharp yellow beak making no cry

recovering quickly
the wolves lope away into the forest

till the end of the day they soldier on through
wet peat bogs
muskeg sucking at their feet
hordes of insects   streams leading nowhere

Silver does not lag

Tawny lets him go ahead of her

exhausted
they finally run into the Asheweig River and follow it

later they rest for an hour
in a cool six-foot-deep polar bear den perhaps centuries old

Silver and Mother lick at his wounds to help them heal

*

by luck at dusk they pick up caribou scent in the bush

in a cold hard wind they soon bed down
gathering strength for the morning

* * *

on their early morning journey through the bush
and along the Asheweig into the Hudson Bay Lowlands
the third largest wetland in the world

they face a cold headwind

and see a big blue sky

piled high with enormous fluffy white cumulous clouds

Silver's wounds are pink and clean and beginning to heal

feeling hunger pangs

the wolves are beginning their fourth day without food of any worth

a pair of sleek wet-whiskered otters follow along with them

swimming effortlessly in the Asheweig River

they would not swim so close

if they knew how hungry these wolves are

but

curious

the otters stop every once in a while to stare

a third of their bodies sticking straight up out of the water

as if they were standing on bottom

wet brown eyes taking the wolves in

also the pack spies a pair of light-grey sandhill cranes

with long pointed grey bills and red crowns on their heads

stalking fish in weedy shallows on the opposite shore

tall bony survivors from the age of the dinosaurs

bobbing their heads to the water

daintily lifting their long thin legs

as if they really didn't want to get their feet wet

into the afternoon the day heats up

and Wolf's pace has quickened

as caribou scent on a new trail grows stronger

several black-headed arctic terns whizz over the river surface

as the wolves cut into the deep bush to follow the scent

*

several miles down the Asheweig River

back from the shore behind a grey outcrop in the shade of balsam fir

six silver-grey adult wolves nap quietly

taking a break from tracking a caribou herd all day in the heat

they only stir to shake off horseflies
or to get up and move to a more comfortable spot

they look very lazy and content there on the dry sphagnum moss
but the truth is every stomach is aching with hunger

out from behind a bush

steps

a huge figure

larger than the others

like them light grey and white on sides and belly

but on her back a dark slate grey

the pack leader

this dignified and beautiful Alpha female makes no obvious signal
but as she heads to the river to drink
the other six arise and follow her

after they all enjoy long slow drinks of cool water
she leads the pack back to the scent

the caribou have circled back southward

to go around some very wet peat bogs and muskeg

along a winding trail

the wolves are in no hurry

this is their territory

they know the routine

they will catch up to the herd and make a kill and eat at last

as the afternoon passes

the caribou scent grows stronger

but these seven are experienced hunters

and although their hearts beat faster

they remain calm and in control

the trail takes a turn north again toward Ghost Lake

and

immediately

the slate-grey Alpha female picks up wolf scent in some fresh scat

and stops dead to investigate

tracks of caribou and wolf and many other animals mingle

hard for her to determine how many wolf
but the wolf scent is fresh and strong

they proceed
with care and quickened interest

in a few minutes
the Alpha female catches a glimpse of a tawny wolf pup
just disappearing around a corner on the trail ahead

the pack fans out into the bush
quickly overtakes the five intruders
chases them as they flee in panic in all directions through the trees

there is no battle plan or pattern to this wild attack

the Alpha female catches the tawny pup by a back leg and turns her over

ahead
wild cries
and the mad scrambling rustle of flight through trees and bushes

the Alpha female abandons the scrappy tawny pup as no threat
and tries to catch up to something of more interest
but all the wolves have disappeared into the bush

she follows the cries of the nearest attack
and finds two males of her pack and a black male fighting for his life
she joins in
and the young black wolf has no chance to escape

any direction he tries he is cut off

the bigger wolves rip at him
and shake him viciously

their weight and strong legs knock him onto his back

the three bigger animals prevent him from getting to his feet
knocking him over at every attempt
and when the Alpha standing over him sees an opening
she thrusts her head in and closes her jaws over his throat

she rips open a fatal wound

the three stand back as the collapsed black wolf gags

on his side he flounders gamely to get up
but falls over
unable to stand

bleeding heavily
in shock from several bite wounds
weakening
finally he goes still

elsewhere
a gangly silver wolf pup
by luck scoots under a rock overhang
too shallow a space for the grey female chasing him to squeeze into

distracted by bloodcurdling cries elsewhere
she takes off

the two leading adults have been separated
but have outdistanced their pursuers

the Alpha male runs west toward Ghost Lake
and the Alpha female flees east

and crosses a narrow stretch of the Asheweig
where it flows over some gravel shoals

mission accomplished
the pack of seven gathers again on the trail
where they stand together and howl wildly

after a few minutes they take up their search for the caribou

late in the afternoon
they locate the herd
single out an adult cow
chase her into the mud of a bog
where stuck knee-deep she is helpless

their blood up
they swiftly bring her down
drag her onto a dry area and gorge themselves
afterward retiring to the trees to sleep

Wolf is still close enough to hear the howling and the kill
so he knows he can safely retrace his tracks

circling around the site where his pack was attacked
he barks quietly

nearly half of all wolf pups do not survive the first year of life
but these pups have been lucky
and within short minutes
Tawny limping slightly and Silver uninjured lope out of the bush
onto the trail where Wolf is waiting

the three animals nuzzle each other
the pups out of control whimpering and pawing at Wolf

Mother does not appear

after mourning over the body of Black
Wolf leads the pups away from the direction their attackers took
in case they should decide to return

later at dusk deep in the bush
Wolf howls briefly for Mother
but there is no reply

in some willows at the edge of a pond
the three survivors curl up and sleep together

* * *

around noon the next day
after labouring around endless bogs and fens and marshes and ponds
being bitten on legs and bellies by blackflies deerflies mosquitoes
they stop to wade and drink in a clear stream
and the three hear the unmistakable chatter of humans

as they carefully approach
they come again onto the shore of the Asheweig River
where the Frog River joins it

on the beach there
five green wood-canvas canoes are hauled up on the gravel

eight young men
tanned and fit
after a summer paddling and portaging across Northern Ontario
accompanied by an adult staffman and an adult Cree guide
are brewing Earl Grey tea and happily enjoying a shore lunch
of peanut butter sandwiches and macaroni and cheese

two young men

just made canoe partners as a change by the staffman

are sitting on a large wooden storage box called a wanigan

getting acquainted

hey new partner

where yuh from?

Mechanicsburg Pennsylvania

you?

Jackson Mississippi

how come the staffman let you keep the mutt?

a yellow lab pup is busily licking peanut butter from the fingers

of the young man from Pennsylvania

nobody can resist those eyes

yer a sucker Pennsylvania

after seven weeks on the rivers he's fun to have around

ya well anything to get you through
I know this is my first summer and my last

will your dad be cool with you quitting?

I'm nineteen
don't imagine he could stop me

did your dad belong to the canoe club when he was a kid?

nope
he decided it would be good for me
so he worked overtime and scraped together some cash

into dope and drinkin'?

school trouble
girls
failing courses
that stuff

discipline will make a man of you

something like that

my dad and his dad both belonged to the club
it's a family tradition
they loved the Great Northern Forest
and took pride in the woodsman's skills

whatever

actually I like the North
it gets in your blood

yer sappy Pennsylvania

grab one end of that wanigan and get in the stern Jackson
the Greenhorn Rapids await

corny name

maybe they named them after us

I just hope we don't die

come here

he lifts the camp mutt into the bow

the two young men carry the heavy wanigan
and place it in the middle of the canoe
toss in the things they're responsible for
two personal packs
the tent pack
and four paddles

Pennsylvania gets in the bow
and Jackson pushes the canoe off the gravel
jumping into his spot in the stern as the craft floats free

the five green canoes
each with two paddlers a wanigan and large backpacks
slide into the Asheweig River

smoothly they glide away from shore
with the rhythmic lifting and dipping of paddles
and quite quickly they are small wavering blurs in the distance
no longer recognizable as humans in canoes
finally disappearing around a corner out of sight

the wolves come out of hiding

enter the abandoned campsite
scout for leavings
and find a large northern pike left behind
which they devour

Wolf allows the pups to eat along with him

just after sunset
having made the mistake of staying too late on the river
trying to reach the Winisk that day
and with not enough daylight left to see well and read the rapids
the canoe club is forced to do something dangerous

shoot the Greenhorn Rapids in the growing darkness

Pennsylvania and Jackson are the first to reach the rushing water
and although in real time they pass through in less than a minute
in their minds time moves in slow motion
and it seems to take forever

in the bow
Pennsylvania sits up high on his knees leans out over the water
pulling hard on his cherrywood paddle
trying to see in the dim moonlight the small curls of white water
that show the location of rocks

he pries his paddle against the side of the canoe
to avoid a dangerous shelf of rock and
pushes the end of the paddle against the dark outline of a boulder
looming above the water's surface

only once do they feel in their legs the vibration
and hear that scary grinding
of rock scraping against the hull of the canoe

shouting directions to Jackson steering in the stern
Pennsylvania guides them safely through

with great whoops of joy
they stand up and punch their fists into the air

they look back
and can see only the dim outline in the darkness of the second canoe
splashing through the last white water of the rapids safely

the twin brothers from New Orleans Louisiana pull up
laughing with relief

three more canoes come through safely

the staffman and the Cree guide last
and there is a happy conference in the middle of the river
where the Cree guide advises the staffman it will rain soon
they should go ashore and make camp immediately

bad luck
a heavy downpour begins before they can get off the river and make camp

so they drag canoes onto the marshy shore

unload hastily

fight their way into the thick wet prickly bush
carrying the heavy packs
sharp branches scratching them and tearing their clothes

erect tents harum-scarum willy-nilly in the dark
laughing and swearing
the beams from their flashlights sweeping wildly through the trees

toss packs in weird-shaped tents that are only half up
roped quickly to trees and bushes
and not too securely either

spread out sleeping bags
and wriggle in with their wet clothes still on

Pennsylvania is happy that his mutt
sopping wet and trembling with fear of the storm
has stuck close and jumped in the tent with them

he immediately dries the mutt off
with a dry towel from the bottom of his pack
and mutt wriggles into the sleeping bag with his pal

after rude jokes and complaints
they all sleep badly in the cold dampness
water dripping on their heads
some tents flat on top of their occupants
rain puddling around sleeping bags and belongings

from across the river out of a dark line of black spruce
they hear the low-moan howling of wolves

the Cree guide remarks to the staffman
they're mourning

*

the sun *does* come up that morning

and they *have* survived

tents and sleeping bags are turned inside out

stretched out and hung up in the trees to dry in the sun

likewise wet clothing and gear

they enjoy an especially hearty breakfast

bacon and large helpings of oatmeal with extra raisins and nuts

Pennsylvania feeds the mutt his own bowl of oatmeal

coffee grounds are dumped into the bottom of a large pot of water

and boiled to make camp coffee

cold hands thankfully cupping hot tin mugs

no griping about the bitterness of the camp coffee

or the grounds in the bottom of the mug

by the time the noon sun is shining strong

all is well and dry

and they break camp

the three wolves awaiting their departure are very patient and quiet
then very disappointed to make a sweep of the campsite
and find no food left behind today

only the tantalizing pool of bacon grease
so mixed with dirt they can't lick it up

the six-month-old pups by now have had enough practice to be useful
but without the help of skilled adults
Wolf has much less chance of bringing down large prey

surviving on small mammals
mostly groundhogs
they continue their journey north
now truly into the Hudson Bay Lowlands
the third largest wetland in the world

their first hours take them through a lush and green black spruce swamp
along the edges of a stream where the blackflies are thick

Wolf leads them to higher drier ground in the poplar trees
where they get lucky and come across a large warren
and kill three rabbits
before they can dive down holes in the rush to safety

the day wears on

and late in the afternoon they walk the high clay banks of the Winisk

stopping once in a while to nap and look down on the river

which moves slowly now with few rapids

it has a mud or gravel shore that will serve them as a nighttime highway

along the river at dusk through a large area of burnout

with the nighthawks zipping around over their heads

stopping in some charred white elm

they see an old lopsided cabin made of rotting hand-squared logs

in an area cleared some time ago

now overgrown with weeds and bushes

from a distance in the elms

they carefully study the cabin

which had not been touched by the fire

then make an approach

around the outside of the cabin there are no tracks

human or animal

but the blueberry bushes have been picked clean

they creep inside slowly
sniff small personal items scattered on the sagging plank floor
shoes and magazines and rusty tin boxes
and on a cot a letter in a yellowed envelope

on the back of a wooden chair with a broken leg
a black and red checked shirt
one arm chewed away up to the elbow
they take refuge there for a nap
Wolf sleeping just inside the doorway facing outward
to protect the pups from sudden intruders

this day
the five green canoes leave behind the marshy shoreline of the Asheweig
and fight a strong headwind to make good progress
forty miles down the Winisk
setting up camp on a stretch of shoreline of steep gravel and mud

they enjoy fresh bread baked in a rough sheet metal oven
and Irish stew from tinfoil packets boiled in water

the mutt is treated to his own portion of stew in a melmac bowl

now all but three of the canoeists are asleep in their tents
glad to have a warm dry sleeping bag tonight

the Cree guide informs Pennsylvania and Jackson
that within three days they will pass the Limestone Rapids
and reach their destination
the new Cree town of Peawanuck

Jackson couldn't help but ask

why a new town?
all the settlements up here are really old

you haven't heard about Winisk?

on May 16 1986
there was a huge spring ice jam
where the Winisk River drains into Hudson Bay

water couldn't get through and backed up four miles
all the way to the town of Winisk

the swollen river caught everybody by surprise
and the deep water had nowhere to go but over the ice and over the town

a sound like thunder

huge chunks of ice smashed through the streets
bulldozing every building except two into Hudson Bay
completely wiping out the town

lots of people injured
two died
my grandfather drowned
and a young mother trying to save her two kids was crushed by the ice

no roads out up here
but somehow the helipad for a helicopter survived

the people of Winisk were stranded in canoes for days
until being airlifted by helicopter to Attawapiskat
by the Department of Indian and Northern Affairs

Winisk was abandoned
and we built a new town

we called this new town "Peawanuck"
meaning "flintstone" in the Cree language

Jackson shook his head

that's amazing!
a whole town wiped out by ice
it's hard to imagine

not to me
I was there
I'll never forget those downed power lines fizzing in the water
and the bang when the power house blew up
I felt the rush of wind on my face

and now we live thirty miles back from the Bay
and on high ground

the guide stands up and stretches back
hands on hips

I'm pooped boys
see you in the a.m.

he slips and struggles noisily up the gravel incline
and retires to his tent

that was one long day

however

we made good progress Jackson

blisters and hard paddling against that goddamn forever wind

does it ever stop?

always coming down off the Bay I guess

you guess

here

have one Pennsylvania

he hands his friend a crumpled pack of Winstons

you make these yourself?

they're all bent

they light their smokes from Jackson's silver Zippo

don't complain big shot or you won't get another one

I don't know why I'm doing this
I don't even smoke

they're good for ya
put hair on your chest and make you a ladies' man

you wouldn't lead me astray would you?

just wait till you wake up with cancer tomorrow morning

looking out over the broad flat Winisk
they sit in silence and finish their smokes .

the northern lights flare up
throw an immense sheer curtain
of pale yellow and lime and wispy white
across the moonlit sky

bedtime   bonehead

as you wish   Mister Mississippi

they douse the glowing coals with water from the big cooking pot

when they awake in the cool morning
and are boiling water for oatmeal and coffee
they see tracks of a large wolf circling their tent
and on the animal highway in the mud of the beach
they see tracks from the night before

two moose
one small bear with a cub
two sets of wolf pup tracks

miles upriver
Wolf and the pups are gorging themselves on a bear cub they killed
after chasing off its very young and inexperienced mother

finished their eating
they wade into the Winisk and enjoy a refreshing drink

following Wolf's lead
Silver and Tawny head into the black spruce to find a sleeping spot

*

bundled up in jackshirts and workpants
the boys break camp and set out paddling
into another day of hard work on the wide Winisk

Pennsylvania
the muscles across my shoulders are so damn tight they're burning
shoot me will yuh?

I wouldn't go to jail for killing a guy like you

man it's cold

the closer to the Bay the colder it will get

this is really fun

*

on the river by noon
the day has heated up a bit
so the boys have stripped down to T-shirts and shorts
and are happier after a shore lunch of hot soup

mid afternoon
a lost gosling adopts their canoe
and wailing pitifully follows them for an hour or so
before he finally gives up and falls back out of sight

what kind of gosling was that Pennsylvania?

Canada goose

how come he was all alone like that?

no idea

poor little bugger

I won't tell anybody I heard you being sentimental

fluff you

*

the remainder of the afternoon
they do a backbreaking three hours of steady paddling
and make good progress blessed with a strong tailwind for a change

the only point of interest on the broad flat river
occurs when they turn a corner
and surprise a mother bear and two cubs eating a pike on the beach

they stop paddling
and watch the mother quickly run with that strong rolling gait
into the bush out of sight with her cubs close behind her

when a storm appears to be brewing up in the western sky
they pull up onshore
unload the canoes
and start to make camp

again on the mud beach they get a shock – very large tracks

Jackson frowns

Oh goody!
polar bear

not scared are you   tough guy?

well now

what if a polar bear comes through the front of the tent tonight?

if a polar bear comes through the front of the tent tonight
I want you to stand up like a true southern gentleman
and fight him to the death

and what will you be doing while I'm busy dying?

I'll be cutting a hole in the back of the tent with my Swiss Army knife

typical Yankee

at that very moment
in a patch of blueberry bushes not far away
as Wolf and pups stand watching several brook trout
zipping around in a cold shallow stream
a half dozen or so cedar waxwings land in the bushes
surrounding the wolves
flit around busily eating their fill of the berries
and disappear in a flurry as suddenly as they arrived

the wolves wade in and try to catch fish

Tawny succeeds in swatting one fat trout onto the bank
and they share a snack
and continue their journey in search of woodland caribou

as a cool evening settles in
both the boys and the wolves are tired and looking forward to sleep

Silver has found a cave in a clay bank of the Winisk
and the two American boys are enjoying a last chat before bed

swiftly
soundlessly
out of the trees
a large white bird with wide wings swoops down
knocks Jackson sideways
scooping his Braves ball cap off his head

Jesus!
what was that?

that was a snowy owl my friend

scared the hell outta me
I didn't even hear him coming

owls fly silently
if you knew anything at all
you'd know they've been doing that for two hundred million years

aren't they tired yet?

very funny

what's he doin' down here stealing my cap
isn't he supposed to be up north in the tundra?

just came down to pay his respects Jackson
are your pants still dry?

the staffman shouts a reminder

get to bed
long day tomorrow

when they awake
a white-throated sparrow is singing sweetly
in the quiet sunshine of the morning
a song that people say sounds like "O, Sweet Canada, Canada, Canada"

a pair of sandhill cranes
like a tall thin fragile grey grandmother and grandfather
with slow careful steps
fish for frogs and crayfish
in the shallows upriver

a balmy morning
no wind yet

a huge osprey
looking very stylish
with two black lightning bolt flashes
etched along the temples of her white head
pulls in her black wings against her white body
drops like a missile
feet first

slap!

hits the river with a great splash
disappears underwater
bursts forth into the clear air
flies away on enormous long wings bent back at the elbows
turning a medium-sized pike headfirst in her claws
as she returns to her high platform nest back in the trees

standing on the beach sipping camp coffee
Pennsylvania and Jackson watch all this

Pennsylvania
what is this
The Garden of Eden?

yes

well I'm Adam
so I guess we know who you are

you're miscast man
more like the serpent

now you've hurt my feelings
suck it up and let's get rolling

*

by now the three wolves
awakened by light
are well into their day's journey
travelling inland from the river

in an area where there is more water than land

looking for caribou sign

Wolf is setting a hard pace

treating the young brother and sister as adults

by noon

the young ones are slowing

so Wolf stops under some trembling aspen for a rest

after a rest

Silver tries to engage Wolf in some play

but he growls angrily making clear he will have none of it

they have seen no caribou tracks

Wolf is serious

and intent on some purpose unclear to them

wolves can smell prey miles away in good conditions

but after they take another rest

unpredictable swirling headwinds make following scent difficult for Wolf

along a stream

flowing out of one of the many small lakes they have passed by today

Wolf sees an animal who at this great distance

seems to be fleeing in panic

by the time the three get close enough

to recognize the animal as a bull moose

he turns off and vanishes into the bush

they never do see who was chasing him

not to be distracted

Wolf continues on his quest

with the headwinds off the Bay the air is much cooler

so they tire less frequently

they stop only once in a while to drink from a pond or stream

beside a pond in a large open area

as they draw close to drink

they see laid out at the water's edge two dry white broken skeletons

of full-grown male caribou

their horns locked together during some past fight in a grip of death

unable to feed or defend themselves
they would have starved to death or been easy prey for a wolf pack

Silver and Tawny sniff around the bones with curiosity

soon after
standing beside Wolf
on the crest of a high grey outcrop
the pups look out
and see suddenly what they have been pursuing so fiercely

two hundred yards across an open bog
three white creatures fishing at the edge of a small lake

a mother
and two year-old cubs

polar bear

the famous white bear
who clawed and chewed to death many explorers
in the arctic seas of earlier centuries

the most feared and deadly land predator in the North

Silver and Tawny are frightened
downwind now getting a strong dose of the rank scent
that was only faint and unrecognizable to them earlier today

Wolf is very still

his gaze focused and intense

watching every move and gesture of the white bears
as they go about their business catching trout in the lake

the sow
for some reason
stands up high on her hind legs
a startling great figure
single and alone there in her height
on the flat brown and green expanse

much taller than any man
tall and woolly and white
looking out over the lake

she turned to face them
her underbelly a light brown
enormous paws crossed over at her chest

she had detected them somehow
a swirl of wind with their scent on it
or a sixth sense
it didn't matter now
the small round black eyes in the white head
pointed right at them

seizing the moment
Wolf charges down the outcrop
and off across the bog

seeing him coming
with the two lanky pups galloping behind
mother bear runs along the lakeshore with her cubs
at an almost lazy pace

catching up to the bears
coming within thirty or forty yards
Wolf sees mother bear look back over her shoulder

she is not afraid of him
but she does fear for her yearlings

although they are as tall as her
they are slender
and would be inexperienced dealing with a strong fierce wolf

she promptly runs into the lake
and dives beneath the surface
followed by her cubs

when the bears resurface they are well out from shore

the wolves stand on the mucky beach
watching intently

Wolf knows these bears must come ashore sometime
but he does an odd thing for him
he howls once in dismay
turns away and leads Tawny and Silver back the way they came
giving up

the three slip away over the ridge of the outcrop
and disappear into the stunted poplars

three white heads continue bobbing across the surface of the lake

leaving a broad upside-down V behind them

and eventually reach the opposite shore

they lumber out

shake themselves

water flying in a wide spray

they continue ambling along the beach in their shuffling style

sniffing for food

an hour later

after having left this lake behind

and walked miles around several other lakes and across bogs and fens

looking up from their feasting on some large trout

they see three wolves within twenty yards

breaking out of a stand of scraggly tamarack

bearing down on them with vicious speed

what happens next is so stirring so terrifying

it is dreamlike

a nightmare in the middle of the day

before they can get very far into the water

the bears are overtaken by the wolves splashing up behind them

the fierce bloodcurdling growls the roaring of the big bear

slashes of enormous paws

ripping of tendons squeals of injury

flashes of red and white and grey

a violent swirl of water and tangled struggling bodies

Wolf succeeds in separating the male yearling from his mother

Wolf lands with weight and force on the bear's back

lunges into his throat as the bear rolls over

the cruel jaws close over the larynx

too late mother pounds Wolf away with one powerful swat

sending him swirling away in a rush of water

the wolves wisely retreat to shore and watch

Silver and Tawny at seven months old

have fought their first deadly battle

and now are licking at the raw red wounds from the bears' claws they refresh themselves with a drink at the lakeside

Wolf ignores his wounds

mother bear

confused and unable to help

watches her male offspring sink in a bloody swirl below the water

she would like to have more of those wolves

but she is experienced enough to know they would quickly run away

as darkness eventually overtakes the scene

Wolf listens carefully

and does soon hear mother and daughter come ashore

and lumber slowly up the beach

beyond hearing

warily the wolves approach the unfortunate young bear

the feeding that takes place is savage

but after a few minutes

satisfied

their muzzles smeared with blood and their bellies bulging

the team of three who were so terrifying and vicious

and such efficient killers

are now quiet

peaceful

and find an isolated safe spot to sleep

Wolf howls for Mother

as he does every night

no reply

*

the canoe club camped on the gravel beach

sit around the big campfire

and savour fresh-baked brook trout

feeling secure

except for the howl of a wolf

and the sight of many polar bear tracks in the mud in front of them

an impressive show of lime-green and lemon-coloured northern lights

and the cat-like calling of the nighthawks swooping overhead

take the boys' minds away from the threat of the bears

and after smokes and jokes they retire to their tents

*

all the next sunny windy afternoon
the boys are paddling with a strong current coursing toward the Bay
but against fierce headwinds and waves churned up by those winds

the mutt decides he will ride between the feet of the Cree guide
in the stern of a different canoe for a change

for as far back as one hundred feet
the bark of trees onshore has been scraped off in the spring breakup
by huge chunks of ice sliding and grinding over the Winisk's banks
propelled toward the Bay by the floodwaters

I'm wearing wool socks
long johns
two pair of workpants
a track top
a flannel shirt
a T-shirt
and a lifejacket
and I'm still cold

mama's boy

remind me again how much fun this is

you'll laugh about this later

if I live

just then they get their first glimpse of the Limestone Rapids
white water stretching across the river
water droplets being thrown into the air off the top of the waves

paddling close to the canoe ahead
they begin to realize the height of these waves
called haystacks
- about four feet -

they are second in line to shoot the rapids

in the canoe ahead
the brothers from Louisiana totally disappear
every time they make it over a wave
and go down into the trough on the other side

here we go Jackson!

they slam into the first wave
and ride up suddenly vertical
water spraying into the bow and over Jackson
and plunge straight down
pointed right at the river bottom

Pennsylvania shouts
hit them straight-on at ninety degrees
or they'll turn us over

they do better on the next wave
hit it square
cut into it cleanly
and down the other side

at the bottom of the trough
Jackson looks up
and can see nothing but haystack in front of him

up and down up and down
over and over

hands tightly gripping paddles

eyes alert

pulling hard on those paddles

hearts pounding

Jackson is very worried

are we going to get through?

not long now

concentrate!

the last three or four waves are getting smaller

until they finally slip into calmer water

I'm glad you took stern today

I couldn'a steered 'er straight head-on like that

we'd 'a tipped fer sure

that was fun Jackson

now it was

they slip into a comfortable pace

turn back and shoreward

stop to watch the other three come through

the next two canoes paddle through fine

no problem

all smiles and safe

the last canoe carrying the staffman and the Cree guide and the mutt

comes riding high on the white crests and disappearing in the troughs

at the final high wave

the mutt decides to climb out from between the guide's legs

and get a better view

his front paws on the gunnel

his bright brown eyes taking everything in

the jerk of suddenly going down into the trough throws him

flying into the waves

one splash and he disappears out of sight underwater
swept along behind

the men curl their canoe around as the waves flatten out
stroke back toward the rapids

Pennsylvania is scanning the water in panic

Jackson is swimming hard toward the centre of the river
straight toward the bobbing blond head
as the pup dogpaddles mightily to stay afloat
eyes casting about in fear

with a few quick strokes Jackson is on the mutt
grabs him by the scruff of the neck
and rolls on his back swimming
with a one-hand backstroke for the canoe
the mutt on his chest

the canoe pulls alongside

Jackson grabs the gunnel with one hand

Pennsylvania crouches low in the canoe

leans over the side

one hand on the gunnel

plucks the mutt from his partner's grip

and deposits the soaked terrified pup in the bottom of the canoe

a great cheer goes up from the boys in the other canoes

Jackson

you're a sentimental fool

shut up

soon

on shore

grins and handshakes

they stand in the gravel and gaze across the river

amazed at a long stretch of high white limestone cliffs

extending for half a mile north and around a bend in the river

a fire is made for their last shore lunch of the day

they raise their mugs to toast the mutt with Earl Grey tea

to Splash!

shouts Pennsylvania

with a dry towel he vigorously dries off the mutt

now known as Splash

long before the canoe club arrives at Peawanuck

the wolves

after a difficult journey of about two hundred miles

have hidden themselves in some black spruce

on the high dusty cliffs just west of the village

they hear the happy voices of the boys as they paddle ashore

at the end of a long hard summer

and watch them run naked with bars of soap in their hands

into the frigid Winisk

jumping out quickly

shouting

gasping for breath

they see Chief Starhunter

walk down the bank to the beach to welcome his visitors

and to make sure

they were not bringing anything into the village he does not want there

the three wolves

ever patient

remain still

and watch the boys put up five tents

in the dusty wind-blown camp west of the village

they watch the light fade to black

and the campfire flicker up

smell the Irish stew and the coffee and the cigarettes

when all is quiet and the village is asleep

as he did months ago in another human settlement far south of here

Wolf walked slowly down the middle of the main street

studying the village

only this time he has two companions

across from the Ministry of Natural Resources office

a small boy

unable to sleep

sits in his mother's lap in a rocking chair

on the front porch of their new house

they notice the three quiet wolves

farther down the dirt street walking away from them

no no you can't pet them

they're wild *wolves*

would they bite me?

no

they would run away from you

are they afraid of me?

no

they could kill us easily

if they wanted to

they just don't like humans

they watch the three wolves walk slowly out of village street lights
into the darkness of the black spruce at the edge of the settlement

*

at noon the next day
Pennsylvania and Jackson are enjoying taking a long time over breakfast
since there is no work and no paddling to do today

when's the plane arriving at the airport to pick us up?

we have no word yet Jackson
all we know is that it's grounded for repairs

hope we get outta this dust soon

all you seem to do is complain

my hobby

let's investigate the village

strolling along the dirt streets of the village
they see about thirty new homes
satellite dishes and teepees
a health clinic a church the Matahamao School
the Nishnawbe Police Station

the Indians they meet are shy but friendly

the boys head right for Chookomolin's store
where they buy cold bottled pop and chocolate bars

walking in the dust blowing along the dirt street
Jackson is greedily enjoying his treats

man this is great
haven't had this stuff for months

remember to brush your teeth back at camp

ok mum

they pass the entire afternoon in the dry hot camp
reading paperbacks snoozing smoking and drinking tea

as the boys start a fire for supper
two shy young Cree girls enter the camp
and show them leather necklaces and T-shirts for sale

Pennsylvania buys a lilac-coloured fleece-lined T-shirt
with three circles printed on the chest
in the larger circle in the centre a picture of Weenusk the Groundhog
in the smaller circles the Canada goose and the polar bear

in an arc over the top of the big circle
the words WEENUSK BAND
and across the bottom
PEAWANUCK ONTARIO

Jackson buys three bead necklaces for three girlfriends at home

one of the brothers from Louisiana
helps the Cree girls with their uncertain English
by discovering they understand his French

the girls relay a message in French from Chief Starhunter
that the boys are invited to his home in the evening to visit
and use his TV to watch videotapes they can rent at the store

this news is greeted with shouts and smiles that embarrass the girls

after supper that night
sitting on the floor of Chief Starhunter's living room
Pennsylvania and Jackson enjoy *Goldfinger*

just as they are getting up to leave
they hear the Chief's radio crackle the news
that their plane has been repaired
and will fly them out to Pickle Lake in the morning

stumbling back to their camp in the complete dark
the boys use the fire made by the staffman as a beacon

would you like me to hold your hand Jackson?

that's for wimps from Pennsylvania

now now
no need to be rude

Splash has heard their voices and comes on the run
slamming into Pennsylvania's shins

whoa there buddy!
your name should be Smash

don't go renamin' him now
you'll get him confused

soon they are zipping themselves up into their sleeping bags
and lying awake
very happy to be heading home

I wonder what the countryside would look like
if we were flying over it right now?

stars twinkling
in the utter darkness over the Great Northern Forest

that's almost poetry Jackson

and don't you forget it

good night

good night

*

Wolf has been pressing the pack hard and
after travelling all night and all morning with little rest
Silver and Tawny decide to have some fun
chasing each other along the shallows of the Shagamu River

Wolf sits resting on a grassy bank
content now because there has been lots of sign of caribou
so in the next few weeks food will be abundant
in the northern range of the woodland caribou

the young ones play until they are exhausted
finally flopping down soaked and panting beside their leader

across the river
as they lie quietly on the shore
appears
a lone dispersing male wolf
who after drinking his fill
raises his head
notices the three and quickly runs up the bank into the trees

a lone wolf
may travel hundreds of miles in search of a mate
but this one has decided not to approach the pack

after a good rest
the pack continues in the direction of the Severn River

they have a bad moment in a spongy wet bog
stopped short by an unfamiliar sight

the partially eaten carcass of a white Arctic wolf covered in maggots
one front paw clamped in a #14 steel-jawed wolf trap
caught trying to eat the bait meat laced with the poison strychnine

they are not tempted to eat

the rest of the day
they have success
killing a number of beaver in the streams
and groundhog on the dry hillsides

they pick a high rocky outcrop to sleep
under a jutting ledge

as they like to do

they watch the sunset in the west

and as he has done every night

since the surprise attack along the Asheweig River

Wolf throws back his head and howls

joined by Tawny and Silver in a chorus of wild discord

miles away

a thin single wolf voice answers

Wolf stands straighter

and howls again more strongly

again an answer

a little closer now

Wolf howls several more times at intervals

but there are no more answers

in about five minutes Tawny and Silver are asleep

but Wolf

still awake and alert

sees not too clearly in the half-light

a single wolf running toward him across the tundra

flowing over the ground at speed like quick water
and as the animal comes within forty yards he recognizes that wolf

Mother

speeding toward them
up the incline of the outcrop

the joyous barking starts
as Tawny and Silver awaken out of their sleep
a fierce pawing and face-licking
circling and jumping
yipping and yipping

a happy tangle of bodies

finally
they quieten down
Wolf and Mother curling up side by side contentedly
Tawny and Silver close at hand

after years of experience
Mother knew the destination of the annual summer migration

and she kept to her solo journey

till a lucky night

the recognizable howl of her mate

hunting caribou will go much better now

with another experienced adult

in the fall

they will retrace their long journey

back to their home territory near the shore of Winisk Lake

and they will have many adventures along the way

some good

some bad

in February or March Mother and Wolf will mate

and about sixty days later in April or May

in her old den where Wolf will not be allowed

she will give birth to four healthy pups

and the adventure of survival will begin all over again

as it must always do

in a lumbering town far away

south of Nakina

a small boy is lying awake in bed

seeing in his mind's eye the powerful grey wolf

smashing down the garage door on top of his father

and escaping through the snow across the backyard

the boy can see the fierce gaze of those yellow eyes

and remember how they seemed human

and he wonders whatever became of that beautiful wolf

* * * * *